THE CHRISTMAS TREE
El árbol de Navidad

A Christmas Rhyme
in English and Spanish

Alma Flor Ada

Illustrated by Terry Ybáñez

Hyperion Books for Children
New York

Printed in Hong Kong by South China Printing Company (1988) Ltd.

First Edition

3 5 7 9 10 8 6 4 2

Ada, Alma Flor.
The Christmas tree / by Alma Flor Ada ; illustrated by Terry Ybáñez
–El árbol de Navidad / por Alma Flor Ada ; ilustrado por Terry Ybáñez.
p.   cm.
Summary: A cumulative rhyme describes the decorating
of the family Christmas tree.
ISBN: 0-7868-0151-4 (trade) ISBN: 0-7868-2123-X (lib. ed.)
[1. Christmas trees—Fiction. 2. Christmas—Fiction. 3. Stories in rhyme.
4. Spanish language materials—Bilingual.] I. Ybáñez, Terry, ill. II. Title.
PZ74.3.A28   1997   [E]—dc20   96-38218

The artwork is prepared using acrylic paint on black paper.

Book design by Edward Miller.

For Daniel Antonio,
may all your Christmas seasons be joyful

Para Daniel Antonio,
que tus Navidades sean todas dichosas
—A. F. A.

For the children of San Antonio

Por los niños de San Antonio
—T. Y.

Daddy brought a Christmas tree.

Papá trajo un árbol de Navidad.

Grandma lights a candle.

Abuela enciende una vela.

Look at the beautiful Christmas tree
with the bright candle
Grandma lit!

¡Qué lindo el árbol de Navidad
adornado con la vela
que encendió Abuela!

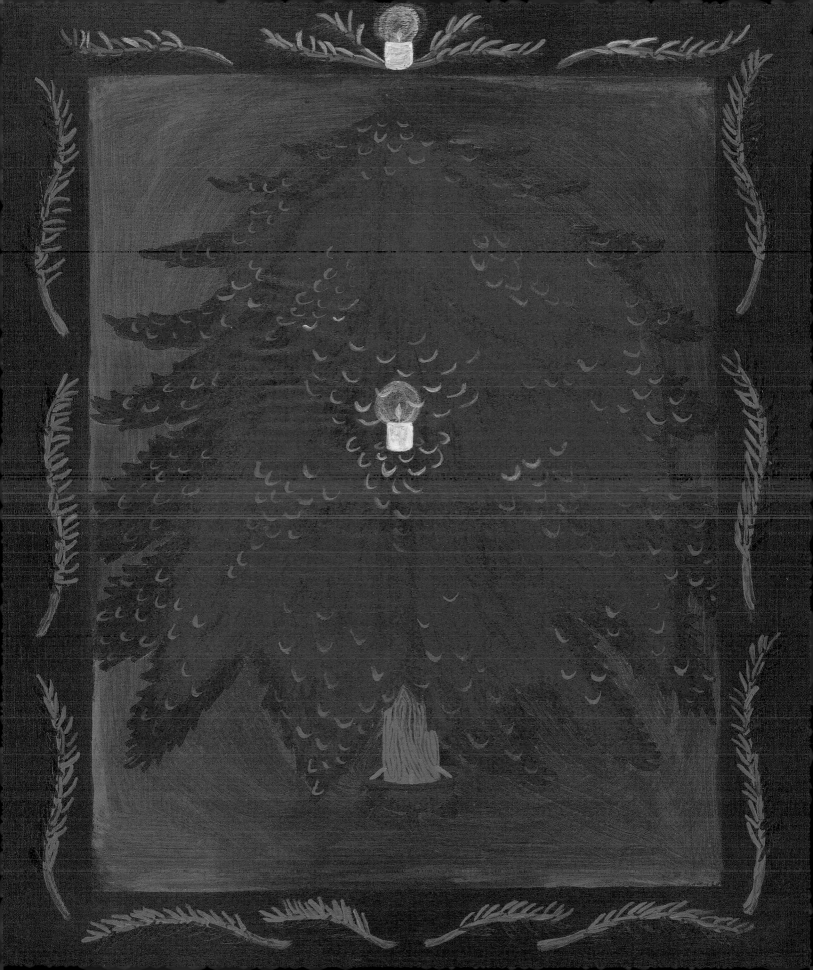

Grandpa hangs a candy cane.

Abuelo cuelga un caramelo.

Look at the beautiful Christmas tree
with the bright candle
Grandma lit
and the candy cane
Grandpa hung!

¡Qué lindo el árbol de Navidad
adornado con la vela
que encendió Abuela
y con el caramelo
que le colgó Abuelo!

Uncle Irineo painted a sleigh.

Tío Irineo pintó un trineo.

Look at the beautiful Christmas tree
with the bright candle
Grandma lit,
the candy cane
Grandpa hung,
and the sleigh
Uncle Irineo painted!

¡Qué lindo el árbol de Navidad
adornado con la vela
que encendió Abuela,
con el caramelo
que le colgó Abuelo,
y con el trineo
de tío Irineo!

My brother Alfonso carved a deer.

Mi hermano Alfonsito talló un venadito.

Look at the beautiful Christmas tree
with the bright candle
Grandma lit,
the candy cane
Grandpa hung,
the sleigh
Uncle Irineo painted,
and the deer
Alfonso carved!

¡Qué lindo el árbol de Navidad
adornado con la vela
que encendió Abuela,
con el caramelo
que le colgó Abuelo,
con el trineo
de tío Irineo,
y con el venadito
que talló Alfonsito!

Aunt Mireya brings the star.

Tía Mireya trae la estrella.

Look at the beautiful Christmas tree
with the bright candle
Grandma lit,
the candy cane
Grandpa hung,
the sleigh
Uncle Irineo painted,
the deer
Alfonso carved,
and the star
Aunt Mireya brought!

¡Qué lindo el árbol de Navidad
adornado con la vela
que encendió Abuela,
con el caramelo
que le colgó Abuelo,
con el trineo
de tío Irineo,
con el venadito
que talló Alfonsito,
y con la estrella
de la tía Mireya!

Mommy is calling us.
Let's go and sing.
We're all so happy—
Christmas is here!

Mamá nos llama.
Vamos a cantar.
¡Qué felicidad—
llegó Navidad!

Author's Note

Christmas was the most extraordinary part of my childhood. A time so wonderful as to be waited for all year. A time with its own particular colors and foods, sounds and smells, a time of surprises and joy.

In Mexico, and in many other Spanish-speaking countries, the days before Christmas are *posadas*, with neighbors singing songs about Joseph and Mary asking for a place to rest. In Puerto Rico, groups of friends knock on each other's doors to sing *bombas*, playful songs new each year. In New Mexico, the streets are lit with *luminarias*, paper sacks filled with sand to hold a candle. All over, Nativity scenes are created with clay figures, *papier-mâché* mountains, mirrors for lakes, and aluminum-foil rivers. Christmas is also a time for *piñatas*. What fun to break them and let out all the candy!

On December 24th, called *Nochebuena*, there is always a big feast. Often Nochebuena ends with Midnight Mass, *la misa de gallo*. And on Christmas Day, the Nativity scene is finally completed with the figure of baby Jesus. In some Spanish-speaking countries, Santa Claus, or *Papá Noel*, leaves gifts for children under the Christmas tree on this day. In other countries, children receive gifts brought by camel from the Three Wise Men, *los Reyes Magos*, on January 6th.

The night of January 5th was my favorite as a child growing up in Cuba. We would always leave grass and water near our beds for the camels of los Reyes Magos. We knew the camels would be tired after delivering gifts all around the world, and hoped that if they would stop to eat and drink, we might catch a glimpse of the generous kings who left us toys and presents, just as they had brought gifts to baby Jesus long ago. Year after year, we were sure we had seen a glittering crown or a purple mantle. And year after year we would promise ourselves that we'd manage to stay awake and talk to los Reyes Magos—but, tired with anticipation, sleep was always stronger than we were.

When my children were little, growing up in the United States, I wanted them to have the same good times as those I remembered. So while they got presents under the Christmas tree from Santa, to whom they wrote in English, on January 6th they also received gifts by their beds from los Reyes Magos, to whom they wrote in Spanish. They were glad to be bilingual! And every year we would travel across the country to spend the holidays with my mother, my aunt Mireya, and the rest of my family—because nothing makes Christmas as special as family does.